Dear Parent:

Congratulations! Your child is taking the first steps on an exciting journey. The destination? Independent reading!

STEP INTO READING® will help your child get there. The program offers five steps to reading success. Each step includes fun stories and colorful art. There are also Step into Reading Sticker Books, Step into Reading Math Readers, Step into Reading Write-In Readers, Step into Reading Phonics Readers, and Step into Reading Phonics First Steps! Boxed Sets—a complete literacy program with something for every child.

Learning to Read, Step by Step!

Ready to Read   Preschool–Kindergarten
• big type and easy words • rhyme and rhythm • picture clues
For children who know the alphabet and are eager to begin reading.

Reading with Help   Preschool–Grade 1
• basic vocabulary • short sentences • simple stories
For children who recognize familiar words and sound out new words with help.

Reading on Your Own   Grades 1–3
• engaging characters • easy-to-follow plots • popular topics
For children who are ready to read on their own.

Reading Paragraphs   Grades 2–3
• challenging vocabulary • short paragraphs • exciting stories
For newly independent readers who read simple sentences with confidence.

Ready for Chapters   Grades 2–4
• chapters • longer paragraphs • full-color art
For children who want to take the plunge into chapter books but still like colorful pictures.

STEP INTO READING® is designed to give every child a successful reading experience. The grade levels are only guides. Children can progress through the steps at their own speed, developing confidence in their reading, no matter what their grade.

Remember, a lifetime love of reading starts with a single step!

Copyright © 2004 by Berenstain Enterprises, Inc.
All rights reserved under International and Pan-American Copyright Conventions.
Published in the United States by Random House Children's Books,
a division of Random House, Inc., New York, and simultaneously in Canada by
Random House of Canada Limited, Toronto.

www.stepintoreading.com
www.berenstainbears.com

Educators and librarians, for a variety of teaching tools, visit us at
www.randomhouse.com/teachers

Library of Congress Cataloging-in-Publication Data
Berenstain, Stan.
We like kites / The Berenstains.
   p.   cm. — (Step into reading. A step 1 book)
SUMMARY: While kite flying one beautiful summer day, Sister Bear and Brother Bear
encounter kites of many different shapes and sizes.
ISBN 0-679-89231-1 (trade) — ISBN 0-679-99231-6 (lib. bdg.)
[1. Kites—Fiction.   2. Bears—Fiction.   3. Stories in rhyme.]
I. Berenstain, Jan.   II. Title.   III. Series: Step into reading. Step 1 book.
PZ8.3.B4493   We   2004   [E]—dc21   2002014879

Printed in the United States of America   First Edition   10 9

STEP INTO READING, RANDOM HOUSE, and the Random House colophon are registered
trademarks of Random House, Inc.

STEP INTO READING®

STEP 1

The Berenstain Bears

We Like Kites

The Berenstains

Random House 🏠 New York

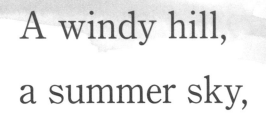

A windy hill,
a summer sky,

a perfect day

for kites to fly.

Running, running
down the hill.

Will our kite fly?

Yes! It will!

More string!

More string!

Let out more string!

We catch the wind!
Our kites take wing!

Kites of every shape
and size

dance across

the summer skies.

Some spin.

Some swoop.

Some loop the loop.

Sad kite, glad kite,

bat kite, cat kite.

A kite with stripes,
a kite with stars,

a kite that wants to
go to Mars.

A fire-breathing

dragon kite

gives the other kites

a fright.

The setting sun
says goodbye.

We reel in our kites
from up on high.

We head for home.

But that's okay.

The hill and sky
are here to stay.

31

And tomorrow is
another day.